Zoe gasped, her heart thudding in her chest. Bertie had waded even further into the lake – and now he was struggling to stay above the water. The little elephant was in big trouble...

Look out for:

Zoe's Rescue Zoo

The Eager Elephant

Amelia Cobb

Illustrated by **Sophy Williams**

nosy crow

With special thanks to Natalie Doherty

To Barb and Neil x

First published in the UK in 2015 by Nosy Crow Ltd
The Crow's Nest, 14 Baden Place, Crosby Row
London, SE1 1YW, UK

Nosy Crow and associated logos are trademarks and/or
registered trademarks of Nosy Crow Ltd

Text copyright © Hothouse Fiction, 2015
Illustrations © Sophy Williams, 2015

The right of Hothouse Fiction and Sophy Williams to be identified as the author
and illustrator respectively of this work has been asserted by them in accordance
with the Copyright, Designs and Patents Act 1988.

Printed and bound in the UK by Clays Ltd, Elcograf S.p.A.

Papers used by Nosy Crow are made from wood grown in sustainable forests.

ISBN: 978 0 85763 375 0

www.nosycrow.com

Chapter One

Meep Gets into Mischief

Zoe Parker wrinkled her nose and squeezed her eyes tightly shut. "Aaaa-chooo!" she sneezed as dust went up her nose. "Aaaa-chooo!"

Zoe was raking up the minty-smelling leaves in the koala enclosure at the Rescue Zoo. All around her, tall green trees stretched up from the dusty, pebbly ground. Every time Zoe moved her rake, a small cloud of dust puffed into the air – and straight up her nose!

As the branches above her head shook, Zoe glanced up. Perched in the tree was Matilda, one of the koalas. Zoe thought she was one of the cuddliest animals at the Rescue Zoo, with her soft grey fur, cute black nose and big fluffy ears. But right now Matilda didn't look at all cuddly – she looked cross!

The koala gave a noisy chatter, and a tiny creature scampered out of the leaves and shot down the tree trunk. He stuck his pink tongue out at Matilda before leaping on to Zoe's shoulder.

"Meep!" Zoe said, grinning at the little mouse lemur. Meep was her very best friend. He was so small he could easily ride on Zoe's shoulder, and he was *always* getting into mischief!

The koala chattered again crossly, and Zoe looked up in time to see her fluffy bottom disappear further up the tree. Zoe giggled. Being with all the animals was her favourite thing about her zoo home, even when they were cross!

Zoe was very lucky – because she *lived* at the Rescue Zoo! Her Great-Uncle Horace was the zoo owner, and knew almost everything about animals. Zoe didn't see him very often, because he spent lots of time travelling around the world, looking for animals that needed help. Whenever he found an animal in trouble or without a home he brought them back to live at the Rescue Zoo! Zoe's mum, Lucy, was the zoo vet, and she and Zoe lived in a cottage on the edge of the zoo.

Matilda shook her furry head and chattered crossly again at Meep, and Zoe smiled. "You're right, Matilda," she replied. "Meep is the naughtiest lemur I've ever met, too."

Living at the Rescue Zoo was the first

exciting thing about Zoe, but the second
thing was *even* more special. Zoe knew a
very big secret: animals can understand
what people say, and talk to them all
the time! But only a few lucky people
can talk back to them. Zoe was one of
these special people. Ever since her sixth
birthday she had understood every growl,
grunt, squeak and roar the animals made!
But she could never tell anyone the
animals' secret – not even her family.

"What were you doing this time,
Meep?" said Zoe as the lemur snuggled
into her shoulder.

"I wasn't doing anything naughty,
Zoe," Meep complained grumpily. "I just
wanted to try one of Matilda's special
leaves. They look so green and juicy, and
they smell so nice. But I had one tiny bite

and then I spat it straight out. It tasted horrible!"

"Oh, Meep!" Zoe sighed. "Those are eucalyptus leaves, and they're poisonous to most animals! They would have made you *very* sick. Matilda can eat them because koalas have special tummies that protect them. She was just trying to help you." She smiled up at Matilda. "Thank you," she told the koala gratefully. "No wonder you were upset with cheeky Meep!"

Matilda nodded her furry head and quickly chattered back.

"No, I'm sure he won't do it again!"
Zoe replied. "Will you, Meep?"

Meep's big golden eyes were wide as he
shook his head. "I'll stick to bananas from
now on. And apples. And maybe nuts too
. . . and sunflower seeds. . ."

Zoe giggled as Meep started listing
all the foods he liked. Meep was a little
animal with a big appetite!

Up in the tree, Matilda suddenly gave
an excited squeak and began chattering
eagerly.

"What is it?" Zoe asked curiously.

"Let's go and see!" chirped Meep,
bounding nimbly back up the tree. Zoe
quickly grabbed the lowest branches and
pulled herself up to where Matilda was
sitting. She wasn't as good at climbing as
the koalas, or Meep, but she was still the

best in her class. She had lots of practice playing with her animal friends!

Peering through the leaves over the top of the wooded enclosure, Zoe saw a bright-yellow jeep rumbling slowly through the zoo gates. It was very dusty, with big muddy wheels, and looked like it had travelled a long way. The back of the jeep was open and flat, without a roof or any seats, and a large wooden crate was strapped on to it.

Around her, Zoe heard lots of noise as the other zoo animals spotted the jeep. The grizzly bears growled curiously. The turtles swam to the edge of their lagoon enclosure. And Oscar, the friendly African elephant, lifted his big trunk in the air and gave a noisy trumpet.

As the jeep got closer, Zoe could see something through the dirt on the door. There was a familiar logo painted there – a hot-air balloon, the symbol of the Rescue Zoo! Zoe's heart gave a big thump of excitement. "It's Great-Uncle Horace!" she gasped. "He's back from his safari trip. And he's brought a new animal for the Rescue Zoo!"

Chapter Two
A Safari Surprise

Climbing down the tree and waving
goodbye to the koalas, Zoe dashed out
of the enclosure and raced towards the
cottage. Meep scampered along the path
next to her. "Goo's back! And there's a
new animal to play with!" he squeaked
excitedly.

They reached the big yellow jeep just

as the door opened, and a huge bird with glossy blue feathers and a curved beak flew out. She swooped straight into the air, happily stretching her wings.

"Kiki!" Zoe grinned as she saw the beautiful hyacinth macaw. Kiki and Great-Uncle Horace were best friends, just like Zoe and Meep, and Kiki travelled everywhere with Great-Uncle Horace.

Then a man with untidy white hair and twinkling eyes stepped out. He wore a crumpled safari hat and jacket, and when he saw Zoe his face broke into a cheerful smile.

"Great-Uncle Horace!" exclaimed Zoe, rushing forward.

"Zoe, my dear! Goodness me, you're getting so big!" cried Great-Uncle Horace, scooping her up for a hug. "I've

been having all sorts
of exciting
adventures in
Africa, but it's
splendid to
come home
and see
you! I've
missed you so
much. And you
too, Meep!" he
added, chuckling
as Meep eyed
the big wooden
crate. "I see your
inquisitive friend
wants to know what's inside!" he said,
winking at Zoe. "You'll both find out
soon, I promise. Ah, here's everyone else!"

A crowd of zookeepers rushed down the path, calling out greetings to Great-Uncle Horace. Then Mr Pinch, the grumpy zoo manager, arrived. His face was like thunder as he spotted the crate.

"Another new animal to make lots of mess! Don't I have enough to do already?" Zoe heard him mutter grumpily.

Zoe's mum, Lucy, arrived next, her face pink from running across the zoo. "Welcome home!" she said warmly, reaching up to kiss Great-Uncle Horace's cheek. Then she saw the crate and grinned. "And who have you brought home this time?"

"A friendly young fellow, who I think will be just right for the Rescue Zoo," said Great-Uncle Horace, beaming. "In

fact, let's show him his new home now.
I'll need a few helpers to put the wooden
crate right outside Oscar's enclosure,
please. Careful though – it's rather
heavy!"

As a group of zookeepers began moving
the crate, Zoe glanced at Meep. The little
lemur looked as puzzled as she felt. The
new animal was going to live with Oscar?
But Oscar was a huge elephant – and
the crate was only the same size as Zoe!
There couldn't be another elephant inside,
could there?

Then Zoe gasped. "Unless," she
whispered to Meep, her eyes shining, "it's
a *baby* elephant!"

Meep gave a squeal and leaped on to
Zoe's shoulders so that he could see better.

"Excuse me, please – coming through."

An elderly man in a zookeeper uniform
rushed over to help.

"If it *is* an elephant, David will be so
happy!" Zoe whispered to Meep.

David the elephant keeper had worked
at the Rescue Zoo for as long as Zoe
could remember, and he was one of her
favourite keepers. He had white hair, a
deep, gentle voice and kind, grey eyes.
Zoe knew that David had always wanted
Oscar to have an elephant friend.

Zoe held her breath as David stepped
forward and opened the latch on the
crate door. The door clattered to the
ground and there was a moment's
silence. Then there was a high, excited
trumpeting sound. The crowd gasped, and
David gave a happy cheer. Zoe couldn't
help jumping up and down. "It *is* a baby

elephant!" she cried.

The tip of a little trunk poked out first, sniffing the air. Then there was a happy squeal and the baby elephant tumbled excitedly out of the crate. He stopped when he saw the crowd, staring curiously at everyone with big brown eyes.

Zoe giggled as he took a few wobbly steps. "He's the cutest thing *ever*!" she said, grinning.

"Baby elephants can start walking on

the day they're born, but this chap needs some practice," Great-Uncle Horace explained. "Normally, the rest of his herd would have helped him to learn, but he was separated from them when he was just a few hours old. He was all alone and very upset when Kiki and I found him. We tried to find him a home at the local elephant orphanage but they didn't have room for a new baby. That's why I decided to bring him back to the Rescue Zoo."

The little elephant flapped his ears happily as he spotted Great-Uncle Horace. He plodded over, raised his trunk, and before Great-Uncle Horace could say a word, the baby elephant reached inside his coat pocket and pulled out a custard cream! Zoe and Meep burst out laughing as he popped it into his mouth and started crunching happily.

"Albert discovered my favourite biscuits on the journey back from Africa," explained Great-Uncle Horace, chuckling.

"Albert? That's a very grown-up name for a baby," laughed Lucy.

"Maybe we could call him Bertie for short?" suggested Zoe.

Great-Uncle Horace's eyes lit up. "Yes, Bertie suits his cheeky little character perfectly! Well done, Zoe."

Zoe grinned as she reached out and stroked Bertie's head. Usually the animals told her their names when they arrived, but sometimes they were so small when Great-Uncle Horace rescued them that they didn't even have a name yet!

"He looks very healthy and happy,"

Lucy said. "Although I wish he'd stay still long enough for me to have a proper look at his ears," she added with a chuckle as Bertie galloped off through the crowd excitedly, lifting his trunk to sniff every single person. "I'll give him a proper check-up later."

"Is he going straight inside his new home?" asked Zoe, glancing at Oscar. The gentle giant had put his huge head over his enclosure fence and was watching curiously.

"We'll have to do it carefully," said David. "Elephants are very kind creatures, but Oscar isn't used to living with a baby. He could squash Bertie accidentally."

Meep gave a worried squeak, and Zoe stroked him soothingly. She knew she could talk to Oscar and tell him to be

extra careful around the new arrival,
but she couldn't tell David and the other
keepers that!

As the grown-ups started talking about
the best way to introduce Bertie to Oscar,
Zoe quickly glanced around. No one was
looking, so she whispered very quietly
to Meep. "We'll have to talk to Oscar as
soon as we can . . ." she began.

But Meep wasn't listening. "Look, Zoe!"
he giggled, pointing a tiny finger.

Zoe turned to see what Meep had
spotted, and her face broke into a relieved
smile. "Mum! David! Great-Uncle
Horace! I don't think there's anything
to worry about," she called. "I just know
Oscar's going to take really good care of
Bertie. Look!"

Everyone turned. Oscar was reaching

his long trunk right over the fence, and Bertie was standing underneath, holding his own little trunk up so that they touched. Zoe listened as Oscar trumpeted.

She grinned. Oscar was *so* pleased to meet Bertie! The other keepers were all smiling too. Only Zoe could understand what the elephants were saying, but everyone could see how happy they were!

Chapter Three
Baby Bertie

"Meep, I'm home!" called Zoe, bursting through the front door of the cottage. She spotted a furry bundle curled up on the sofa and smiled. "Meep, have you been snoozing all day?"

A tiny head popped up, and Meep blinked sleepily. "I was just resting my eyes, Zoe," the lemur explained, yawning.

"I wasn't *really* asleep."

Zoe grinned. "Come on – I'll get changed out of my school things and then it's time to go and see Bertie!"

Zoe had rushed home from school as fast as she could. She'd even decided not to stay late for her Monday-night drawing club, which she normally loved. She'd been desperate to get back to the Rescue Zoo – and all because of a very cute baby elephant!

All weekend, Zoe had tried to talk to Bertie. She always made sure she spoke to new animals when they arrived at the zoo, so that she could try to help if they felt nervous or frightened. They were often very surprised that a little girl could understand them! But yesterday there hadn't been a single second to speak to

Bertie on his own.

First, David had taken Bertie into his new enclosure so that he could meet Oscar properly. Bertie had been so excited, he'd rushed around in dizzy circles, trumpeting noisily! Then Lucy had popped in to give the little elephant a proper check-up. It had taken a while, because Bertie thought she had come to play chase, and cheekily ran away from her as she hurried after him. After that, Great-Uncle Horace and Kiki had come by to say hello. Zoe waited and waited, but before she knew it, it was time to go home for tea!

"It might not be as busy today though," she told Meep hopefully as she put on leggings, a red top and a cardigan, and fastened her paw-print-charm necklace around her neck. "Let's go!"

They ran along the path, calling hello to their other animal friends as they passed. But as they drew closer to the elephants, Zoe noticed a funny noise in the air. It was a bit like the buzzing she heard whenever she visited the Rescue Zoo bees. "What is that?" she asked, frowning.

The funny buzz grew louder and louder. They reached the next corner, peered round it – and both stared. The noise was the chatter of an enormous crowd outside the elephant enclosure! Zoe had never seen so many people in the zoo before, all talking eagerly about one animal.

"The baby is *so* adorable!" cried a lady with big sunglasses.

"Elephants are my favourite!" called a

boy in a blue jumper, holding his camera
up to take a picture.

"Look how many people want to see
Bertie!" Zoe whispered in amazement.

"How will we get in, Zoe?" Meep asked
anxiously.

"Don't worry. We'll use my special
necklace!" Zoe replied, reaching for
the paw-print charm around her neck.

It was very precious to Zoe, because it had been a present from Great-Uncle Horace. It opened every door and gate in the whole zoo, and meant that Zoe could visit any animal whenever she wanted.

"Excuse me," said Zoe politely, making her way through the crowd. She dodged past a family taking pictures with their phones, and squeezed through a huge group of girls and boys in Brownie and Scout uniforms who were standing on their tiptoes to see Bertie. "He's so cute!" one of the Brownies cried. When Zoe reached the fence, she held the charm against a panel on the gate. With a quiet click, it swung open. Zoe and Meep went inside and shut the gate behind them.

"Wow," a little girl breathed, staring at Zoe. "I wish I could do that!"

The elephants' home looked just like the real African savannah, with lots of tall acacia and apricot trees. David was holding out a big handful of peanuts for Oscar, who was using his clever trunk to scoop them straight into his mouth, without even taking the shells off. Bertie watched Oscar hopefully.

"He's just had a bottle of milk," David told Zoe. "He'll need to drink around fourteen litres of milk a day, but he'll be eating more and more solid food as well. I don't think he's hungry, he's just eager to do whatever Oscar is doing!"

Zoe giggled as Bertie watched Oscar eat, his ears waggling with excitement.

Oscar carefully used the tip of his trunk to push a peanut over to the little elephant. Zoe giggled as Bertie dropped

the peanut straight away, chasing after
it with his trunk, but Oscar patiently
showed Bertie how to pick it back up and
pop it in his mouth.

Zoe smiled as Bertie rushed up to her. His tasselled tail was swishing excitedly, like a happy puppy's. As he trumpeted hello, she was even more desperate to talk to him. But David was right there – and all the visitors were watching!

Suddenly Meep gave a noisy chatter. He hopped off Zoe's shoulder, ran across the enclosure and leaped on to David's arm – grabbing a peanut right out of his hand! The crowd started laughing as Meep scampered all the way up Oscar's trunk and perched on his huge, grey head, where he nibbled cheekily on the peanut.

Zoe grinned. Her funny friend was distracting everyone for her! As the crowd took pictures of the naughty lemur, she bent down and whispered quickly in Bertie's ear, "Hello, Bertie!"

Bertie's eyes lit up and he gave an loud squeak. Zoe could tell he was trying his best to be quiet, but he was too excited!

"I'm glad Oscar told you about me," she replied quietly, smiling. "Oscar is one of my best friends here at the Rescue Zoo. And I hope we're going to be good friends too. We can't talk properly with all these people around – but I'll come back as soon as I can. I promise!"

Bertie nodded eagerly and reached up to nuzzle Zoe's face with his little trunk. It felt very soft and velvety, and Zoe couldn't help giggling. David looked over and chuckled. "Is Bertie up to mischief again?" he called.

Zoe laughed. "Mum says our new elephant is a little bit naughty."

"He's not naughty, he's just eager to be involved with *everything*!" David said with a smile.

Zoe saw Bertie's eyes light up. The baby elephant wiggled his tail and lifted his trunk in the air. Then he started stomping his feet on the ground, and rushed around the enclosure excitedly. But he wasn't

looking where he was going! Zoe held
her breath as he crashed straight into
one of Oscar's huge legs, twirled around
dizzily . . . and tumbled over in a heap!

Meep laughed so much he nearly fell off
Oscar's head. Zoe and David rushed over
to check Bertie was all right – but Oscar
had already wrapped his big, strong
trunk around Bertie's tummy to help him
get back on his feet, and then patted his
head gently. Zoe giggled as Bertie raced
straight off again, already looking for
more fun. Rescue Zoo's newest arrival
was a real bundle of energy!

Chapter Four
Weigh Day!

"Walnuts for the parrots?" Lucy asked.

"Check!" Zoe replied, putting them on the table.

"Oranges for the chimps?" said Lucy.

Meep struggled to hold up a whole orange. "Check!" Zoe giggled.

"Then I think we're ready for Weigh Day!" Lucy smiled.

Weigh Day was one of Zoe's favourite days in the Recue Zoo calendar. Once a year every creature in the zoo was weighed, so that Lucy and the keepers could make sure that they were all fit and healthy. It was a good way to tell if the tiny marmosets were growing big and strong, or if the greedy pot-bellied pigs were getting a bit too tubby! Lots of the animals didn't like standing on the special weighing scales, so Zoe always helped out on Weigh Day, rushing from enclosure to enclosure, giving each of her animal friends a treat and whispering encouragement to them.

"Mr Pinch wants to meet with everyone before we start," Lucy said, pulling a funny face. "He'll talk for a while, so why don't you go and visit Bertie before we begin? I know you've been longing to see him."

"OK!" Zoe happily agreed. "I—" She paused as her nose tickled, then she sneezed, one, two, three times in a row.

"Are you OK?" her mum asked, sounding concerned.

"Yes — I'm fine." Zoe grinned, blowing her nose. "I can't wait to find out what Bertie's been getting up to!"

"I'll meet you at the ring-tailed coatis," Lucy told her.

Zoe grabbed her coat and rushed outside with Meep. It was so early that the zoo wasn't open to visitors yet. A whole week had passed since the little elephant had arrived at the zoo, but Zoe had been working really hard on a special homework project so she hadn't had much chance to visit Bertie again. Zoe couldn't help feeling sad when Great-Uncle Horace had come round and chuckled about Bertie tying his own trunk in a knot, and when Mum told her how Bertie had trumpeted noisily at some ducks flying overhead, making them all quack with surprise!

Zoe turned the corner and skidded to a halt as she heard a familiar voice. "Gather round, everyone!"

Meep froze on the zoo pathway just ahead of Zoe. "Mr Pinch," Zoe whispered. Meep carefully padded three steps backwards, then turned and leaped quickly on to Zoe's shoulder.

"Mr Pinch sounds really bossy today," Meep whispered in her ear. "Let's hide!"

Zoe sighed. "But we have to go past

him if we want to get to the elephants!"
she pointed out.

Meep scampered ahead and peered
round the corner, then ran back over to
Zoe.

"Mr Pinch is with all the keepers," he
chattered. "Maybe if he's busy talking, he
won't notice us?"

"OK," Zoe agreed. "Let's try to slip past
quietly."

Zoe tiptoed up to the sprawling oak

tree just ahead and peeped round it.
Mr Pinch was making an announcement
to a group of zookeepers. He was holding
a long list of all the animals in the zoo,
with an empty box next to each name.

"As you know, today is Weigh Day!"
He frowned grumpily, adding, "No doubt
the animals will be messing around even
more than usual. Any bad behaviour
should be reported to me immediately!"
He nodded importantly.

As Mr Pinch barked orders at the keepers, Zoe and Meep sneaked past and rushed to the elephant enclosure. When they arrived, Zoe used her necklace to open the gate and they slipped inside.

"Morning, Oscar! Morning, Bertie!" Zoe called as they walked over to the elephants, waving.

Bertie squealed excitedly when he saw Zoe and Meep. His ears flapped and his dark eyes lit up, and when Zoe reached out to stroke his head he ran around her in a ring until he wobbled dizzily. Zoe burst out laughing, and even Oscar gave a deep, booming trumpet of laughter.

"You're very happy this morning," Zoe said, smiling at him. "Are you glad to see us?"

Bertie nodded and swung his trunk from

side to side, making a happy squealing sound.

"Silly Bertie, you haven't been waiting to talk to me for *months*," said Zoe, grinning. "You've only been here for a week!"

Meep squeaked with laughter. Bertie gave another earnest little trumpet.

"It *has* been a very busy week, Bertie," Zoe agreed kindly. "I hope you're enjoying being here at the Rescue Zoo?"

Bertie waggled his ears excitedly. He was so eager to tell her how much he loved the zoo that he stumbled over his own feet and almost fell down! Zoe beamed as the baby elephant told her all about his enclosure, his big best friend Oscar and all the kind people who had been to see him. But she hesitated when

Bertie told her that he wanted to see the whole zoo for himself, and visit all the other enclosures.

"I'm not sure about that, Bertie," she said. "All the other animals at the Rescue Zoo are very friendly, but some of them are quite shy. They might not like an elephant stomping through their homes – even a baby one!"

Bertie looked so sad that Zoe quickly added, "But David sometimes takes Oscar on a walk around the zoo to get some exercise. You can see inside the other enclosures from the path. Maybe we could do that again soon, and you could come too!"

As Zoe mentioned Oscar's name, Bertie looked round for his big friend. Oscar was standing nearby, curling his trunk up to eat leaves from tall tree. Bertie trotted over to him and tried to copy him, reaching up as high as he could go, trumpeting loudly and twisting around Oscar's legs. Oscar looked down at him patiently, his mouth full of leaves. Then Oscar slowly walked over to a small tree with low branches, with Bertie trotting after him. Zoe smiled as she realised that the big elephant had

taken Bertie there so he would be able to
reach the juicy green leaves by himself.
But Bertie took one look at the tree,
shook his head stubbornly, and dashed
back to the tall tree that Oscar had been
eating from. Bertie gazed up at the tree
and gave a hopeful trumpet.

"Bertie, it's lovely that you're so proud
to be friends with Oscar," Zoe laughed.
"But you can't eat from the same huge
trees as him, just because you want to be
a big elephant, too! The smaller tree will
be much easier for you," she explained.

But Bertie shook his head stubbornly.
So Oscar curled his trunk all the way
round a high branch, pulled off a trunkful
of leaves and passed them down to Bertie.
The little elephant happily took one leaf
at a time and put them into his mouth,

then squealed for more.

"Cheeky Bertie!" giggled Zoe. At least Oscar didn't seem to mind his mischievous friend. The big elephant had a twinkle in his gentle brown eyes as he watched Bertie munch his breakfast.

The enclosure gate swung open and David walked in, smiling. "Morning, Zoe. You're here nice and early! We've come to weigh the elephants. I thought Oscar could go first, then Bertie will see there's nothing to be worried about."

Behind him, a big red tractor was rumbling slowly into the enclosure. Zoe could see one of the other zookeepers, Will, sitting in the driver's seat. The Rescue Zoo symbol was painted on both doors and it was pulling a huge silver weighing scale on a trailer behind it. The zoo needed an extra-specially big scale to weigh Oscar, as well as the rhinos and the hippos, because they were so heavy.

"Could you park over there, Will?" David called, pointing to a spot in the middle of the enclosure. "I'll just run back and shut the gate."

As David jogged back over to the gate, Bertie stared at the digger in amazement. For a moment, Zoe thought he was frightened. But then he gave an excited squeal and rushed towards it as fast as his little legs could carry him. "Bertie, slow down!" Zoe hissed anxiously, chasing after him. "That's really dangerous!"

Bertie was heading straight for the huge wheels of the digger, trumpeting happily. The baby elephant thought it had come to play with him! "You're going to get squashed, Bertie!" Zoe called desperately.

But Bertie was too excited to listen.

"Bertie, I've thought of a new game!" Zoe shouted, thinking fast. "Chase me instead! I bet you can't catch me."

Bertie turned round straightaway,

his ears wiggling happily. Suddenly, Zoe
wasn't sure this was such a good idea.
Bertie was an *elephant*, after all – and he
was charging straight towards her! She
started running away from the digger,
so that Bertie moved out of the path of
its huge wheels. She was fast, but the
elephant reached her in no time. *Thump!*
Bertie thudded playfully into her, flinging
his trunk around her waist for a big hug.

"You win, Bertie!" Zoe laughed, trying to catch her breath. "But maybe that's enough for now." Bertie might be a baby but he was still very strong, and he was already much heavier than her.

At least he didn't get hurt, she thought, relieved to see that the digger had stopped. It was slowly lowering the massive scale on to the ground. Bertie looked at it curiously, then poked Zoe's hand with the tip of his trunk, wanting to know what it was. "It's to weigh you, so we can see how heavy you are," Zoe whispered. "Don't worry, it's really easy! Look, Oscar's going to go first."

Bertie watched as Oscar began lumbering steadily over to the scale. Then the baby elephant gave a sudden trumpet and rushed towards it. Oscar stopped and stared in surprise as Bertie scampered under his huge feet, hopped on to the scale and squealed proudly.

Zoe and the keepers burst out laughing. They hadn't needed to worry about how they'd persuade Bertie to climb on to the scale. The funny little creature was so eager, he had done it all by himself!

Chapter Five
Wriggly Ringo

When Zoe and Meep left the elephant
enclosure, they were both still giggling
at Bertie pushing ahead of Oscar. Zoe's
giggles made her cough, and Meep had
to pat her on the back with his paw!

"Thanks, Meep," Zoe said, as soon
as she could talk again. "Bertie was
so funny."

"He wants to do whatever Oscar does!" Meep agreed.

"He's a very eager elephant," Zoe said with a smile. "At least that's one animal who's already been weighed today! Come on, let's find Mum and see if we can help with the others."

They hurried through the zoo towards the ring-tailed coatis. In every enclosure there was a keeper trying to get the measurements for Weigh Day. There was lots of splashing in the sea lion enclosure. The slippery sea lions were jumping out of their pool and into a special sling, which was attached to some scales. Zoe was surprised at how well they were behaving, until she noticed their keeper was throwing a silvery fish to each sea lion once it had been weighed!

Next door the tiny possums were being placed gently into a set of scales no bigger than a teacup. Just the tips of their ears peeped out over the top as their keeper wrote their weight down on a notepad.

There was a lot of grumbling coming from the next enclosure. Zoe giggled as she spotted Mr Pinch trying to make the baboons line up neatly as they waited their turn to be weighed. He raced around frantically, tripping over his own feet as he tried to shoo them into place. But as soon as he managed to put two baboons next to each other and turned his back on them, they tumbled out of line, rolling playfully on the ground or leaping up into the trees, hooting cheekily.

"Naughty things!" Mr Pinch cried

furiously, his cheeks growing redder and
redder. "Now I've got to start all
over again!"

"Zoe, there you are!" called a voice
from across the path. Great-Uncle Horace
was with Lucy in the ring-tailed coati

enclosure, looking a bit flustered. The sleeves of his safari jacket were rolled up to his elbows and his safari hat was perched crookedly on his head. In his arms was a very wriggly animal.

"The coatis don't want to be weighed," explained Great-Uncle Horace.

The ring-tailed coatis were some of Zoe's favourite creatures. They had orangey-red coats, pointed snouts, gorgeous dark eyes, and bushy tails that were striped black and white. Their enclosure was covered with tall poles and ropes for them to climb on. Lucy and the coati keeper, Auriol, were holding up tasty snacks to the coatis to try and tempt them down, but it wasn't working!

"We've been chasing them round for ages," Great-Uncle Horace continued, "but they just won't sit still! Could you hold Ringo while we try to round up the others?"

"Of course!" Zoe replied, using her paw-print charm to open the gate. She carefully lifted Ringo out of Great-Uncle Horace's arms and held him gently. Checking that Great-Uncle Horace, Lucy and Auriol were busy trying to catch the others, she bent down and whispered to him. "It won't hurt, you know, Ringo! It's really quick and easy. All you have to do is sit on that funny box for a second, and then there'll be a nice tasty treat for you."

Ringo's ears pricked up when he heard about the treat, and he squeaked a question. Zoe nodded, smiling. "Yes, all your brothers and sisters can have one too. They have to be weighed first though!"

Ringo squeaked again, loudly this time, and all the other coatis stopped to listen. Auriol's mouth dropped open in surprise as they scurried towards the scale and lined up neatly, waiting for their turn. Zoe lifted Ringo on to the scale first, then gave him a cuddle once Great-Uncle Horace had marked his weight down on the chart. "Well done, Ringo," Zoe whispered, grinning as she handed him a juicy strawberry to nibble.

"Good work, Zoe," Lucy grinned. "I don't know how you do it!"

Zoe and Meep grinned at each other. "Who's next on the list, Mum?" Zoe asked Lucy.

"Bella the polar bear," Lucy replied.

"Ooh, good!" Zoe said with a smile. "I want to see how much bigger she's grown since the last time she was weighed!"

But as they started packing up their things, a grumpy voice snapped from further down the path. "These animals make me so cross! Why can't they just all behave themselves and sit on the scales properly?"

Zoe and Meep ducked behind Great-Uncle Horace as Mr Pinch marched past the coati enclosure and stomped into his office.

"I hope he stays in there all day," Zoe whispered to Meep, which made the little lemur snort with laughter.

Suddenly a huge trumpeting noise boomed through the zoo. It was coming from the elephant enclosure – and this time it didn't sound very happy! "Quick, Meep!" whispered Zoe, scooping up her friend and rushing towards the noise.

"I wonder what Bertie has done now!" Meep chattered.

"That's not Bertie," Zoe told Meep in dismay. "It's Oscar!"

Chapter Six
Oscar's Watery Worry

Zoe and Meep rushed back along the
path, past the groups of visitors who were
streaming into the zoo. They passed two
boys who were racing along on matching
silver scooters.

"I wonder what that elephant was
trumpeting about!" Zoe heard one of
them say as he whizzed past.

"He was really noisy!" the other boy agreed, giggling. Just then, the trumpeting sound floated down the path once more. *What's happening?* Zoe wondered again, dashing through the gate and into the elephant enclosure.

Bertie was racing around, his ears flapping. Oscar was standing alone at the back of the enclosure, trying to make himself as small as possible against the fence. David was next to him, stroking his huge ears.

"Is Oscar all right?" Zoe called, running over to them. "Didn't he want to be weighed?" she asked. Usually Oscar didn't mind Weigh Day because he was always proud to hear that he was the heaviest creature in the whole zoo.

But David shook his head. "No, that

was the easy bit! He stepped on to the scale without any fuss, just like Bertie. I gave them both an orange as a treat for being so good. Then . . ." David sighed. "I thought it might be fun to get out the paddling pool, so that Bertie could have a splash about. But Oscar saw me going to fetch the hose and got very upset."

"Oh!" Zoe was beginning to understand what the unhappy trumpeting noise had been. She knew that Oscar looked big and brave but that he was *really* frightened of water. He hated baths, and he even hid under the trees when it was raining heavily!

David sighed. "I've never known an elephant to be scared of water before. Usually, splashing around in water holes with the the herd is one of their favourite things to do! Your great-uncle and I think something must have happened to him when he was a young elephant, still living in Africa. You know the famous saying about an elephant's memory, don't you?"

"Elephants never forget," said Zoe, nodding. "Poor Oscar."

Zoe had talked to Oscar lots of times about why he didn't like water. At least, she'd *tried* to talk to him. The big, gentle creature wouldn't explain where his fear came from. Whenever Zoe asked him, he just shook his head firmly and refused to tell her anything else.

Meep gave a tiny snort. "I think Oscar is right. Getting wet and cold and drippy is horrid!" the little lemur announced with a cheeky chatter. "I like to stay nice and dry."

David looked at the paddling pool again and scratched his head. "Why don't we fill the paddling pool up for Bertie anyway? If Oscar sees Bertie splashing around—"

"He might realise there's nothing to be worried about!" finished Zoe, grinning. "And I bet Bertie paddling will be the cutest thing ever."

David unrolled the long rubber hose and attached it to a tap. Then he used it to fill up the paddling pool so the water was just a few centimetres high. Bertie heard the splashing noise and came over to have a look. He stared at the twinkling water, then curiously dipped the end of his trunk in.

Bertie's eyes opened wide and he gave a squeal of excitement. Without a moment's

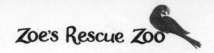

hesitation, he lifted his legs over the side
of the pool and plunged straight in! Zoe
and David laughed at the little elephant
as he plodded around happily, blowing
bubbles with his trunk and splashing
water everywhere.

Zoe looked over to see if Oscar was watching, but the big elephant was still hiding behind a distant clump of trees, as far away from the water as he could get. Zoe felt sad. She didn't want Oscar to be scared!

Bertie seemed disappointed that his big friend wasn't coming to play with him. He barged out of the paddling pool, sending water sloshing everywhere, and marched over to Oscar.

When Oscar backed away from the soggy little elephant, shaking his head crossly, Bertie's ears drooped sadly and he trotted back over to Zoe.

As David went to comfort Oscar, Zoe gave Bertie a little hug. He blinked and waggled his trunk.

"Oh, Bertie! Oscar does love you," Zoe replied. "He just doesn't like water that much."

Bertie trumpeted sadly.

Zoe stroked Bertie's big ears softly. "I promise you'll never be left alone again. Here, *I'll* play in the paddling pool with you." She bent down and ran her fingers through the cool water, then splashed some at the little elephant. Bertie brightened up immediately, and sloshed back into the paddling pool happily

Then Bertie sucked some water up with his trunk with a noisy slurping sound. He turned to Zoe and Meep, and pointed his trunk towards them.

Uh oh! thought Zoe. But before she could say a word, Bertie sprayed the water right at her!

"Ooooh!" squealed Zoe. "I'm soaked!"

Still, she couldn't help laughing. Bertie was just so eager for his new friends to play with him!

Meep, though, was not very pleased. "*I* don't like getting wet!" the tiny lemur grumbled, shaking out the droplets of water from his fur.

But even Meep couldn't stay cross with Bertie for too long. The little elephant was just having so much fun!

Squish! Squelch!

"My shoes are making a funny sound," laughed Zoe as she and Meep walked back to the cottage later. After they'd emptied the paddling pool Oscar had gone back to being his friendly self. David had told Zoe that he was going to take the elephants for a walk round the zoo tomorrow, and he'd promised to wait until Zoe was home from school so she could go too.

They'd had a brilliant afternoon playing in the paddling pool with Bertie, but now Zoe's head was aching a bit and she was glad to be home.

As they went inside and through to the kitchen, Zoe suddenly sneezed again and again.

"Bless you!" said Lucy, turning round from where she'd been chopping up some carrots for dinner. "You were sneezing earlier on as well. Are you feeling all right?"

"I don't know. I feel a bit funny, Mum," said Zoe.

"You look a bit pale, love." Lucy put her hand against Zoe's forehead. "And your head feels hot. Let's take your temperature."

She went to the kitchen cupboard and pulled out a first-aid box, then popped a thermometer in Zoe's mouth. She left it for a couple of minutes and then checked the reading. "Oh dear, you've got a temperature. I think you'd better hop straight into bed and I'll bring you up some medicine."

Zoe put on her blue dolphin pyjamas and climbed into bed. She normally hated going to bed early, but today she felt too sleepy to complain. Her throat felt sore now, and her nose was tickling even more. Her mum brought her a box of tissues and a bottle of medicine, and Zoe swallowed two sticky spoonfuls. Then her mum tucked Zoe's covers round her and drew

the curtains. "I would have made you a
hot water bottle, but you have Meep to
keep you toasty!" she said, stroking Zoe's
head. "Poor Zoe. Get some sleep now, and
I'll be downstairs if you need anything."

"What about school?" Zoe asked croakily. "And I'm taking Oscar and Bertie for a walk tomorrow. I can't miss that!"

"Let's see how you're feeling in the morning," said Lucy, switching the light off. "Then we can decide if you're well enough, OK? Night night."

As Zoe closed her eyes she felt Meep snuggling up next to her, his furry little body very soft and warm. The last thing Zoe heard before she drifted off to sleep

was his tiny voice whispering in her ear.
"I'll look after you, Zoe," Meep promised.
"You'll feel better soon!"

Chapter Seven
Zoe's Day Off

When Zoe woke up the next day she yawned, stretched, then glanced at the panda clock on her bedside table. Then she looked at it again, feeling very confused. It was almost lunchtime!

"Meep, what's going on?" she said, sitting up in bed. "I'm late for school!"

Meep was perched by her feet, wide

awake. "You were still poorly, so your mum decided you needed to stay in bed!" he chirped. "She rang up school and explained you were having the day off. She keeps peeping through the door to see how you are, like when she checks on the animals at the zoo hospital! Goo and Kiki came too. Goo tucked your blankets round you so you were extra snug. But I've been taking the best care of you," he added proudly.

Zoe was still a bit sniffly but her shivers had gone away. Apart from her bunged-up nose, she felt fine! She went downstairs and into the kitchen, realising her tummy was rumbling. She took some biscuits out of the cupboard, and just as she was popping one into her mouth, Lucy walked through the front door, her special vet bag slung over her shoulder.

"You're awake!" she said, kissing Zoe's head. "How are you feeling?"

"A lot better," Zoe said, taking a big bite of biscuit. "I was asleep for hours!"

Lucy looked at her watch. "Well, it's too late to go to school now. I think you can go out into the zoo for the rest of the day and get some fresh air. But I want you to take some more medicine first, and you're not to get wet again! And stay away from the cold enclosures, please. No visiting Bella today, or the penguins."

Zoe nodded happily, winking at Meep. Suddenly she was excited – she had a whole extra afternoon to spend at the zoo, and she'd still get to go on the walk with Oscar and Bertie! As Lucy set off to visit a baboon with a poorly eye, Zoe quickly ran upstairs and got dressed, being careful to wrap up warm. Then she and Meep headed out into the zoo, stopping to chat to their animal friends along the way.

One of the first enclosures they passed belonged to Harold the hyena. Harold padded straight up to the fence and gave a friendly bark. "Thanks, Harold! I feel

much better today," replied Zoe, smiling.
"But how did you know I was poorly?"

"That was my idea," Meep told her
proudly. "When Goo and Kiki came to
visit you, I asked Kiki to fly around the
zoo, telling all the animals you weren't
very well. We've thought of lots of ways to
help you feel better!"

Harold wagged his tail eagerly. The
funny hyena explained that laughter
was the best medicine, so Zoe should try
listening to one of his jokes. "OK then!"
said Zoe, grinning.

Harold barked his joke and waited
hopefully. "Hmm, I don't know that one!"
said Zoe, thinking. "What kind of fish
only swims at night?"

Harold barked the answer – and started
screeching with laughter! Zoe giggled too.

"A starfish! That's funny. Thanks, Harold. I do feel better!" she told him.

As Zoe and Meep carried on walking through the zoo, all her animal friends wanted to ask how she was feeling. Lots more tried to give her helpful tips too. The sloths, Peggy and Pepper, sleepily advised

her to get plenty of rest, before closing
their eyes and starting to snore noisily.
And the baby hippo, Hetty, suggested she
sit down in some squishy mud, because
doing that always made her feel better!

Zoe grinned and pulled Meep into her arms for a cuddle. "I'm not sure I like the idea of a mud bath," she whispered, giggling. "But having all my animal friends around is making me feel lots better."

Zoe stroked Meep's soft fur and gave him a kiss on the top of his furry head. "Now I *really* can't wait to take Bertie round the zoo and let him meet everyone properly!"

Chapter Eight
The Elephant Stroll

As Zoe got close to the elephant enclosure she spotted David inside, putting fresh straw in Oscar and Bertie's cosy shelter.

"Hi, Zoe!" he called, smiling. "How are you feeling?"

"Better! I would have hated to miss Bertie's first walk," Zoe explained.

David nodded. "I thought we could take

them to the water-lily lake. Bertie can paddle in the shallow water, and maybe we could convince Oscar to try it too!"

"Bertie's going to be so excited to go for a walk round the zoo!" Zoe whispered to Meep. "And I think he'll love the lake."

"But, Zoe, do you really think Oscar will want to have a paddle?" Meep asked, frowning.

Zoe shook her head. "No, I don't! But there are lots of nice trees around the lake, and mud for him to cool down in, so I'm sure he'll have fun anyway."

Zoe went with David to get some treats for the elephants, to help keep them from wandering off on their walk. Zoe knew she could tell Bertie which way to go – but she was sure he'd like some treats too! Meep scampered ahead eagerly, and when they arrived back at the enclosure, the tiny lemur had already told the elephants to get ready for their walk. Oscar looked very pleased, and Bertie was so excited he was racing around in circles!

David walked ahead of them to clear the path through the zoo, and Zoe strolled between Oscar and Bertie. For every five steps she took, Oscar took just one slow, giant step. Zoe could feel the path shake beneath her feet as the huge creature plodded along next to her. Bertie kept rushing to look inside each new enclosure they passed.

Lots of the other zoo creatures grunted, squeaked or roared hello as the group walked past. Oscar and Bertie raised their trunks to say hello back. After a few minutes, Bertie turned to Oscar and Zoe and gave a puzzled squeal.

Zoe giggled. "You haven't seen any animals with trunks like yours, Bertie, because there aren't any! Only elephants have them."

Bertie shook his head in disbelief, but Oscar nodded gently, agreeing with Zoe. The little elephant trumpeted again curiously.

"Well, I use my hands to pick things up, and Meep uses his little paws," Zoe explained. "Some animals have strong jaws and teeth to carry things, like the lions and tigers. The pelicans use their clever bills to scoop up fish. And some animals carry everything they need on their backs, like the tortoises. Every creature is different."

Bertie stretched out his trunk in front of his face and gave a noisy toot. He was even more proud of his trunk now that he understood how special it was!

The zoo was busy now and the visitors they passed couldn't believe their eyes as the funny group walked by. Zoe beamed proudly as they pulled out their cameras and phones to take photos.

"Can I touch the little one?" one very tiny girl asked shyly.

"Of course!" Zoe said. Leaning forward, she whispered, "Hold still!" in Bertie's ear. The girl giggled as she softly patted his head – then laughed delightedly as the baby elephant curled his trunk round her middle for a hug.

Suddenly a voice snapped, "David, there you are! I've been looking all over for you!"

"Oh no," grumbled Meep as Mr Pinch marched over. "Why does horrid old Mr Pinch always spoil the fun?"

"I need to discuss the results from Weigh Day with you," Mr Pinch continued bossily. "Come to my office, please. It will only take a moment." He shot Zoe and Meep a mean look and added, "And then I'd like to know why certain people are not at school on a school day!"

David hesitated, then nodded. "Will you be all right, Zoe? Carry on and I'll catch you up in a minute or two. Don't lose any elephants," he teased, grinning.

Zoe smiled back as David and Mr

Pinch disappeared down the path. She wasn't sure she could ever manage to lose something so big!

Zoe waved to some other visitors and watched as David and Mr Pinch strolled out of sight.

Walking through the zoo with *two* elephants was even slower than walking with just Oscar! All the visitors wanted them to stop and have their photo taken with Oscar and Bertie.

"We're never going to get to the lake!" Meep chattered in Zoe's ear.

"Let's take a short cut through the hippo enclosure," Zoe suggested as they passed the enclosure door. "I'm sure Hetty the baby hippo would love to meet baby Bertie!"

She pressed her special paw-print

necklace to the door and led the two
elephants inside.

The hippo enclosure was a big, flat
pasture full of grass for the hippos to
eat and a big muddy lake for them to
wallow in. Zoe shaded her eyes from the
sun and saw the shapes of all the hippos,
Humphrey, Hilda, Helena and baby
Hetty, some in the pasture and some in
the lake, their heads just poking out of the
water like big rocks.

When he saw the glittering water,
Bertie trumpeted loudly in excitement.

Before Zoe could stop him, the little
elephant trotted straight to the water's
edge to dip his feet in, and started
splashing around playfully.

"Bertie, no!" Zoe called. "That's not the
water-lily lake, that's the hippo lake. It's

quite deep and I don't think they want to be disturbed by a baby elephant. Please come out!"

Oscar hung back near the enclosure fence, eying the water nervously. "It's OK," Zoe said as she turned to soothe the old elephant, stroking his warm ears and patting his trunk.

But Oscar just looked more and more nervous. Suddenly he looked over Zoe's head and gave a huge trumpet. Zoe heard the alarm in Oscar's call and whirled round. She gasped, her heart thudding hard in her chest. While she wasn't looking, Bertie had waded even further into the lake – and now he was struggling to stay above the water. The little elephant was in big trouble!

Chapter Nine
A Watery Rescue

Zoe watched in horror as Bertie waved his trunk desperately in the air. He was wriggling and splashing around, trying to swim to safety, but something was wrong.

Bertie gave a frightened trumpet and Zoe gasped. "Meep! Bertie's stuck in the mud!"

The little elephant was struggling in the

water, splashing and thrashing as he tried to get free.

Meep squealed with fear, and Oscar let out another bellowing trumpet. Zoe had to do something, and fast!

"Bertie! This way!" she shouted, waving her arms. "Head to me!"

But Bertie was panicking so much, he didn't even seem to hear her. Zoe looked around desperately.

"I have to go in after him!" she said, starting to pull at one of her shoes.

"You can't, there are hippos in there!" Meep squeaked in alarm.

Zoe knew that none of the animals at the Rescue Zoo would want to hurt her, but she'd never swum with the hippos the way she could with the dolphins and other animals. It was too dangerous.

"I have to do *something!*" Zoe gasped.

She grabbed a branch from the ground and pulled it up to the edge of the lake. Meep grabbed the end too, and together they held it out, getting it as close to Bertie as they could.

"Bertie!" Zoe called. "Grab this!"

Bertie saw the branch and reached his trunk out in the right direction, but he was too far away.

Zoe held the branch out as far as she could, but it was no good. Water was going in Bertie's eyes and up his trunk, and he coughed and spluttered as he tried to keep his head above water.

"Someone help!" Zoe shouted, looking around desperately.

Then she heard an enormous splash. Oscar had jumped into the lake! Zoe stared in amazement as the big elephant strode through the muddy water. "Oscar's coming, Bertie!" she cried, clinging to him. "Just hang on!"

When Oscar was close, he stretched out his massive trunk towards the little elephant. Bertie reached out, his small trunk twisting round Oscar's huge one. With a great squelching sound, Oscar pulled Bertie out of the sticky mud.

Then he started walking
backward, towing Bertie closer
to the shore with every step.
Finally they reached the edge
of the water, and Oscar pulled Bertie out.
"Bertie!" Zoe flung her arms around
the elephant, and so did Meep, who for
once didn't mind that Bertie
was dripping wet. Zoe took
some big, deep breaths.
She felt very shaky
but she was so happy
that Bertie was safe!

The little elephant seemed just as
pleased to be out of the water as Zoe
was. He shook like a dog, then pressed up
against one of Oscar's huge front legs, his
trunk curled around it, hugging Oscar
as hard as he could. Oscar was stroking
Bertie's head with the tip of his own trunk

and speaking to his young friend in a gentle, reassuring rumble.

Bertie hugged his big best friend, then came over to nuzzle up to Zoe.

Zoe smiled. "You don't have to say sorry, Bertie," she told him, cuddling him back. "I know you just got overexcited when you saw the water."

Bertie gave a tiny, nervous trumpet and Zoe shook her head quickly. "Oh no, Bertie, of course you don't have to leave the Rescue Zoo! This is your home for ever, no matter what.

We all love that you're an eager little
elephant but we just want you to be safe.
So when we get to the water-lily lake,
you should stay in the shallow water until
you get a bit bigger. OK?"

Bertie nodded, wrapping his trunk
around Zoe's middle to give her an
elephant hug.

"It's just lucky Oscar was there," Zoe sighed. "And that he was brave enough to come into the water to get you."

She reached up to pat the huge elephant's side. "Will you tell me why you were so frightened of water?" she asked softly.

Oscar hesitated for a moment, then trumpeted shakily. Zoe listened as he told the story: how he fell into the river when he was a tiny baby himself, and was quickly swept away. "You can't have been much older than Bertie," gasped Zoe, and the big elephant nodded. "So that's how you lost your family."

"No wonder you didn't like getting wet!" chirped Meep.

Zoe beamed at her huge friend. "But you rescued Bertie, even though you were frightened," she told him. "That was the bravest thing I've ever seen, Oscar."

"Me too!" chirped Meep, and Bertie waggled his ears eagerly in agreement. Oscar gave a happy trumpet – and Zoe burst out laughing. "The water actually felt nice?" she repeated in amazement.

"Well, maybe you and Bertie can go swimming more often – just not with the hippos!"

Chapter Ten
Bertie Gets the Sniffles

Three days later, Zoe and Meep were
about to have a race along the zoo path.
It was just getting dark and most of the
visitors had already gone home. "Ready
. . . set— Naughty Meep, you're supposed
to wait until I say 'go'!" Zoe yelled,
giggling as Meep sprang ahead of her.

Zoe's cold was completely better now.

After her adventure with Bertie and Oscar, she'd been worried that her cough and sniffles might come back worse than ever. But she felt fine and the next morning she was ready to go back to school.

"Can't catch me, Zoe! Can't catch me!" chattered Meep cheekily, darting nimbly past some visitors who were clustered outside the giraffe enclosure.

Suddenly the mouse lemur stopped and cocked his head to one side, listening. "What's that funny sound?"

It was a very strange, squeaky, snuffling noise

– and it was coming from the elephant enclosure. *What's Bertie up to now?* Zoe thought, reaching for her paw-print charm and opening the gate.

Inside, David was kneeling down next to Bertie, patting the tiny elephant's back reassuringly. Oscar stood close by, watching over his friend. And to Zoe's surprise, her mum and Great-Uncle Horace were there too.

Lucy was rummaging around in her vet bag. "It's in here somewhere!" she said, and finally pulled out a silver stethoscope. She put the earpieces in and listened to Bertie's chest.

"Mum! Great-Uncle Horace!" Zoe called, rushing over. Suddenly she felt worried. "What's going on? Is Bertie all right?"

Right at that moment, a noisy sneeze exploded from Bertie's trunk! The little elephant jumped in surprise, looking all around him. "That was the funny honking noise we heard before, Zoe," giggled Meep.

"I don't think Bertie knows what a sneeze is," whispered Zoe, grinning back. Great-Uncle Horace and David were chuckling too. "There's nothing to worry about, love," Lucy told Zoe, smiling as she packed her stethoscope away. "Bertie's caught a cold, just like you! It's not serious though. He'll be back to normal in a day or two. He just needs some rest and lots of healthy food."

"And perhaps the odd custard cream," whispered Great-Uncle Horace, winking at Zoe.

"I think it's time the cheeky little thing went to bed," added David. "Zoe, do you want to help me tuck Bertie in?"

"And then it's time for our dinner! Great-Uncle Horace and Kiki are joining us tonight too," Lucy told Zoe.

Zoe grinned. "Brilliant!"

Oscar and Bertie were cuddled up in their cosy shelter, in a warm bed of fresh

hay and grass. David had even fetched
some fluffy blankets to make sure Bertie
was extra snug. Zoe helped the baby
elephant curl up and then covered him
with the blankets, so that just his head
and trunk were peeping out.

"Sleep tight, Bertie!" Zoe whispered.
"I promise you'll feel much better soon.

Meep and I will come back tomorrow to see how you're getting on. And Oscar's here to take good care of you!"

As Zoe, Lucy and Great-Uncle Horace left the enclosure, with Kiki flying overhead and Meep scampering in front of them, Mr Pinch came marching up the path. "What is that honking noise?" he snapped.

"I am trying to do some very important work in my office and I can't be disturbed!" he announced, pushing past them and going into the enclosure. "I'm going to tell that naughty little elephant to keep the noise down!"

Great-Uncle Horace chuckled as they carried on walking home. "Something tells me Mr Pinch will wish he hadn't done that. . ." he told Zoe, his eyes twinkling.

A minute later they heard another sneeze from behind them – and a huge, angry yell. Zoe bit her lip so she didn't start laughing as Mr Pinch barged past them again. His face was red and his smart and usually spotless zoo manager's hat was splattered with little drops.

"Elephant snot!" he cried, marching

back to his office. "Yuck!"

Meep giggled so much that he almost fell over. Great-Uncle Horace, Lucy and Zoe managed to hold it in until they got

back to the cottage. They rushed in, shut the door, glanced at one other – and burst out laughing. "That was so funny," gasped Lucy, shaking her head.

"Ah, poor Mr Pinch," chuckled Great-Uncle Horace.

Zoe grinned widely and hugged Meep. "Good old Bertie," she added happily.

The Rescue Zoo's eager little elephant was just as mischievous as ever – but she wouldn't change him for anything!

Look out for more amazing animal adventures at the Rescue Zoo!

The Rescue Princesses

Have you read them all?

nosy crow